PATSY CLINE'S
WALKIN' AFTER MIDNIGHT

Judith A. Proffer

WITH

Julie Dick Fudge

★

Illustrated

BY

Yoko Matsuoka

Patsy Cline's Walkin' After Midnight

Judith A. Proffer with Julie Dick Fudge

This book was produced with the cooperation and approval of Patsy Cline Enterprises, LLC

Copyright 2024 Morling Manor Music Corporation (o/b/o Operating Unit, Meteor 17 Books) and Patsy Cline Enterprises, LLC

Cover and interior art by Yoko Matsuoka

Art direction by Judith A. Proffer

Cover and interior design by designSimple

ISBN 979-8-8693-5559-1

Printed in the United States of America

METEOR 17
— BOOKS —

www.meteor17.com

To the sweet dreamers
who keep Patsy's memory, music,
and dreams alive

Say hello
to Little
Patsy Cline.

"Hi y'all."

Patsy has a BIG voice,
a BIG heart, and

Great Big

Shiny Dreams.

These aren't
ordinary dreams.
Patsy dreams
of one day singing
onstage at
Carnegie Hall.
And in
Las Vegas.
And at the
Grand Ole Opry
too.

She dreams of being in
the Country Music
Hall of Fame
and Museum in
Music City,
Nashville, Tennessee.
A pretty fancy dream
given there isn't even
a museum there (yet)
when she dreams it.

And when she's feeling
**especially bold
and daring**
~ a Patsy thing to do ~
she imagines
having her
very own
museum there
one day too.

Patsy's sleep dreams
are also
big and bold
and can be
**quite colorful,
weaving wonder**
soon after she tucks in
every night.

Some nights
in her dreams
Patsy climbs
high upon a
twisty willow
to get a
better look
at things.

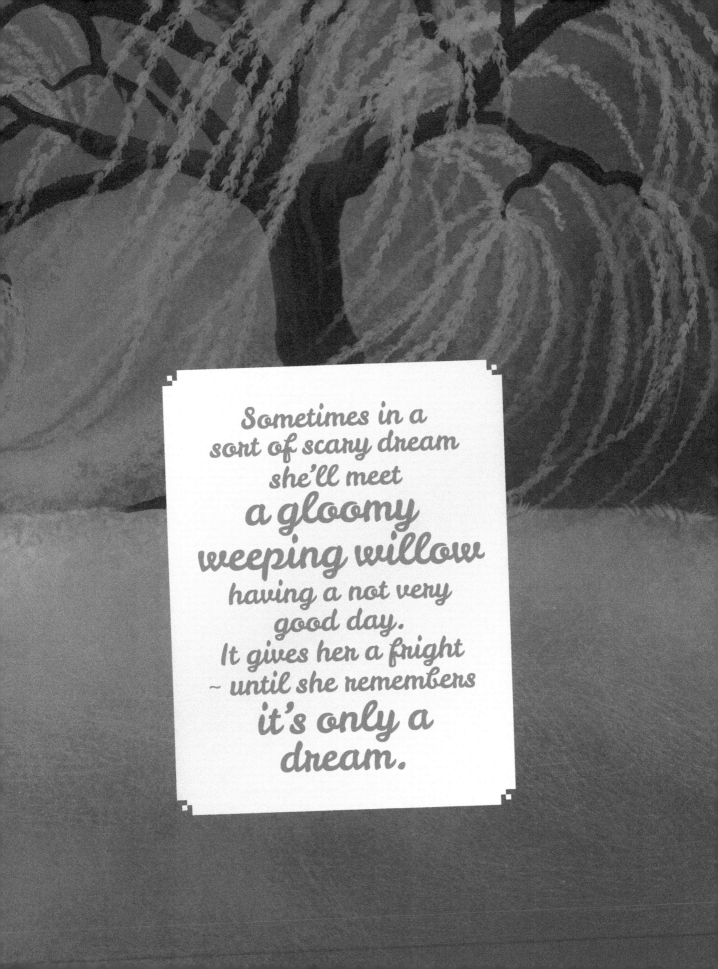

Sometimes in a
sort of scary dream
she'll meet
**a gloomy
weeping willow**
having a not very
good day.
It gives her a fright
~ until she remembers
**it's only a
dream.**

And,
because
she's Patsy,
she enjoys
sweet
dreams
too.

Some of Patsy's favorite dreams are her **daydreams.** That's when she's wide awake and **her mind wanders away** from the things she should be doing.

Like
sewing
a showy
something
to wear at
the Opry.

And fizzing
*ice cream
drinks*
at the
soda shop.

Or
piddling
in the
garden.

And when she takes a little break
from her chores
Patsy daydreams
that she can hear her own voice
swirling around her in the air.

But her
**very favorite
dreams of all**
are the dreams
that happen
after midnight.
It's when Patsy goes
dream walking.

Deep down,
she knows that
she's fast asleep
and yet, somehow,
it all seems
so very,
very real.

Which is especially
wonderful when your
dream walking
after midnight dreams
allow a loved one
to visit your heart.
Like Patsy's dog,
Pepe.

Pepe died after he lived an
extra long very good life.
And even though he lived an
extra long very good life,
it made Patsy quite sad
to say goodbye.

PEPE

Until one night
deep in her
after midnight sleep,
Patsy is dream
walking near a
lonely willow when
Pepe appears
by her side,
chasing away that
sad feeling.

Her heart leaps
and she tells him about
all of her daydreams
and sleep dreams and
walking after midnight
dreams too.

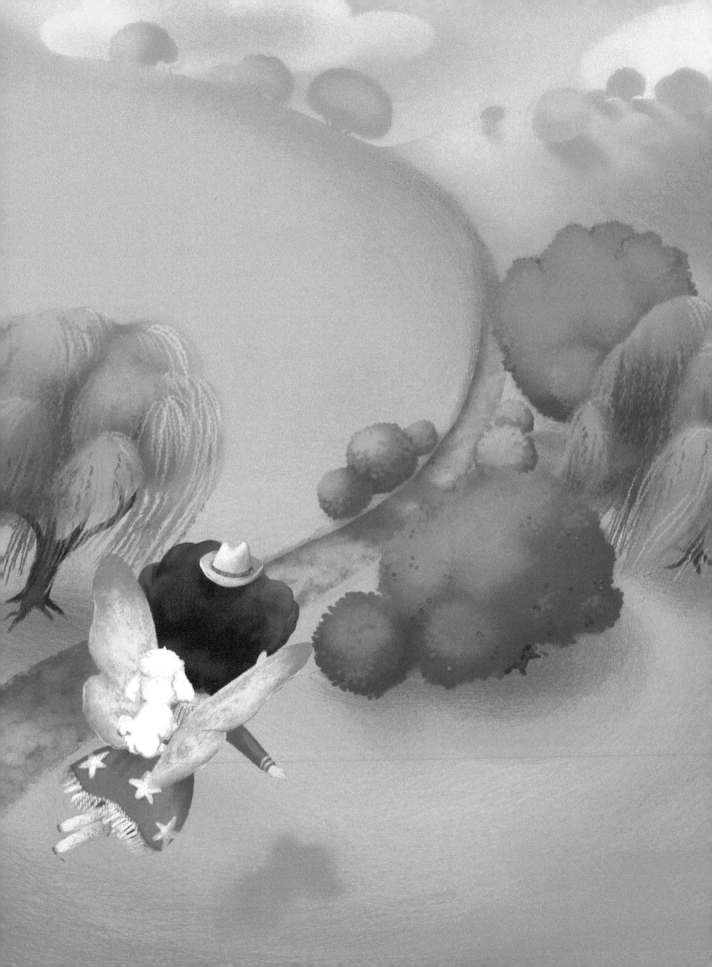

The next night when she
dream walks
after midnight,
she and Pepe soar
over the hills of
Virginia.

Another night
they share an
ice cream soda
and she tells Pepe
some Little Patsy stories.
Like when she won
a tap dancing
contest at only four
years old and how
her nickname was
"Ginny."

Some nights
they sit in
the garden
enjoying music,
side by side.

Other nights they play
hide and seek
in the sky,
and Patsy almost always
hides on the
moon.

Pepe doesn't dream walk with Patsy every night. **Some days she sees him in the clouds** when she's daydreaming about other things.

And some days
she searches for him
in daydreams and
sleep dreams and
dream walks after
midnight and she
can't find him
anywhere.
Patsy knows dreams
can be like that.
They can be tricky
and messy and silly
and charming and
sometimes feel much
too far away
to grasp.

But some dreams can feel so real that you can tuck them inside **your heart** to visit and cheer you when you need it most.

And if you have a big heart and big shiny dreams like Patsy, dreams can come true. Sometimes it just takes a little time and a bunch of patience.

And a nice long dream walk after midnight.

Printed in the USA
CPSIA information can be obtained
at www.ICGtesting.com
CBHW040755040824
12579CB00006B/45